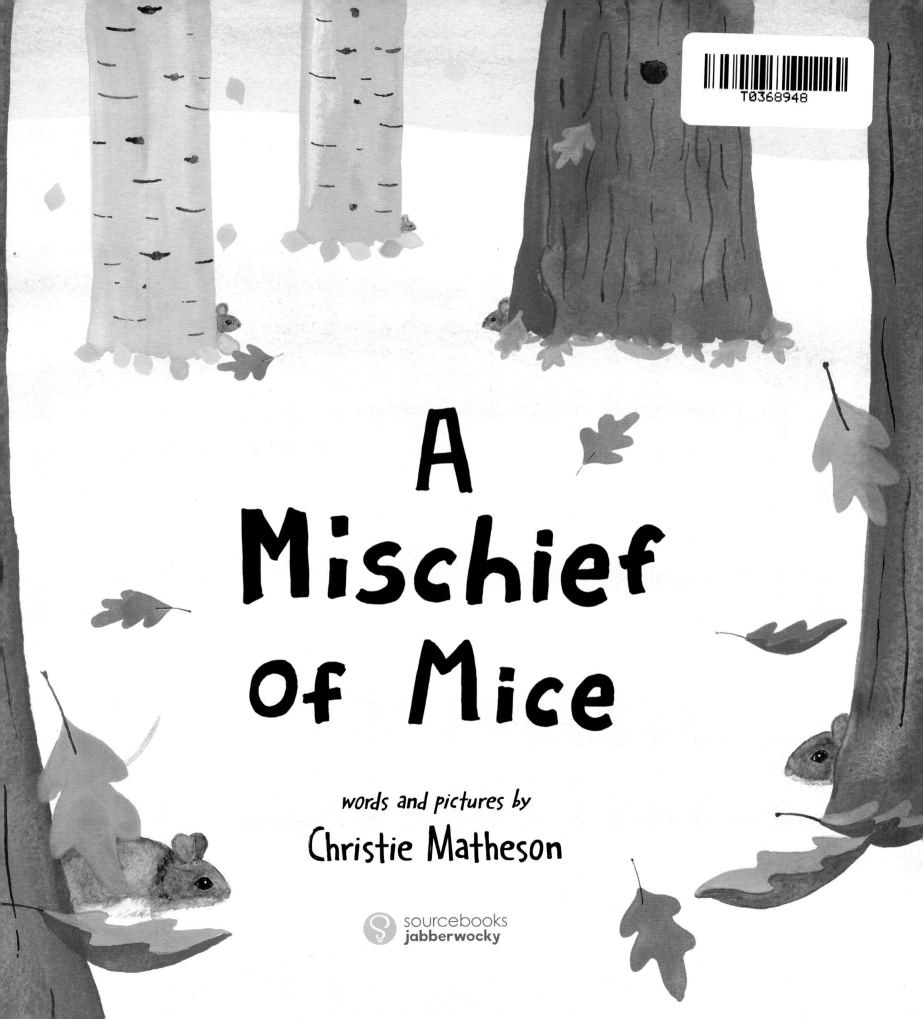

A Mischief Of Mice

words and pictures by
Christie Matheson

sourcebooks
jabberwocky

For Will.

Copyright © 2024 by Christie Matheson
Cover and internal design © 2024 by Sourcebooks
Cover and internal design by Jordan Kost/Sourcebooks

Sourcebooks and the colophon are registered trademarks of Sourcebooks.

The full color art was created using watercolor on paper.

Published by Sourcebooks Jabberwocky, an imprint of Sourcebooks Kids
P.O. Box 4410, Naperville, Illinois 60567-4410
(630) 961-3900
sourcebookskids.com

Cataloging-in-Publication Data is on file with the Library of Congress.

Source of Production: 1010 Printing Asia Limited, Kwun Tong, Hong Kong, China
Date of Production: March 2024
Run Number: 5038541

Printed and bound in China.
OGP 10 9 8 7 6 5 4 3 2 1

A mischief of mice used to play in these woods.

Then one dusk they just...

disappeared.

"What happened?" worried a scurry of squirrels.

"We could be next!"
they feared.

A skulk of foxes slunk about

as the eerie wind shrieked and blew.

Watching it all was
a gaze of raccoons.

The squirrels wondered
what those raccoons knew.

A clutter of spiders
dangled from their
webs, each hanging
by a thread.

When the squirrels asked the spiders if they'd seen the mice, they simply shook their heads.

An unkindness of ravens lurked in a tree.
Did they scare the mice away?

The squirrels heard strange chatter.
Was something the matter?

No.
Just a party of jays.

As night-time fell, the squirrels spied, on a roost, an ominous parliament of owls.

Perhaps,
the squirrels thought,
the owls are to blame.

Then a band of coyotes howled.

Did the coyotes know who took the mice?
Or were they just howling at the moon?

Soon a cauldron of
bats flapped overhead,
screeching a spooky tune.

Those bats are creepy!
They took the mice!

That's what the silly
squirrels thought.

The squirrels, it turned out,
were wrong about this.

The truth is the bats did not.

A prickle of porcupines ambled by,
ignoring everyone they passed.

One of the squirrels risked
getting poked.

(In this case, it *could* hurt to ask.)

"Have you seen the mice?"
the brave squirrel said, reaching
out with a tentative tap.

"The mice? I don't care," said the prickly 'pine.

"It's cold, and I'm going to nap."

"A nap?" mused the squirrels, shivering in the wind.

"A nap surely does sound nice."

"But we can't go inside. We can't and we won't. Not 'til we find the mice!"

Just as the squirrels were about to give up, full of angst and despair, who came along to help solve the puzzle?

It was a sleuth of bears!

"The mice have gone missing!"
the squirrels exclaimed.

"Where, oh where,
could they be?"

"Don't fuss," said the bears.

"Let's follow the tracks."

"Aha! They lead right to this tree."

Sure enough, there
were tracks,

and soon the squirrels saw that
no one had done the mice harm.

"You see?" said the bears. "It's a cold night. They've just gone inside to keep warm."

A Collection of Collective Nouns

A group of mice is called a MISCHIEF. Mice can climb many different surfaces, jump a foot (30 cm) in the air, run *fast*, and even sing!

A group of squirrels is called a SCURRY. Squirrels bury acorns to hide them from pesky food thieves, but they don't dig them all up—meaning they help trees grow!

A group of foxes is called a SKULK. Foxes are often solitary animals, but if you do see a group, it's probably a family, including a mother fox and her cubs.

A group of raccoons is called a GAZE. They are nocturnal animals, which means they are mostly active at night. And they can see very well in the dark.

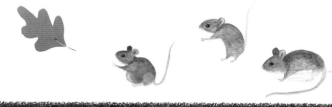

A group of spiders is called a CLUTTER. While most spiders are solitary animals, they can also work together to build large communal cobwebs.

A group of ravens is called an UNKINDNESS. But they can actually be very kind—they make friends with each other and display empathy.

A group of jays is called a PARTY. They make a lot of different noises, including some that warn other birds when predators are coming.

A group of owls is called a PARLIAMENT. Owls have special feathers that help them fly silently.

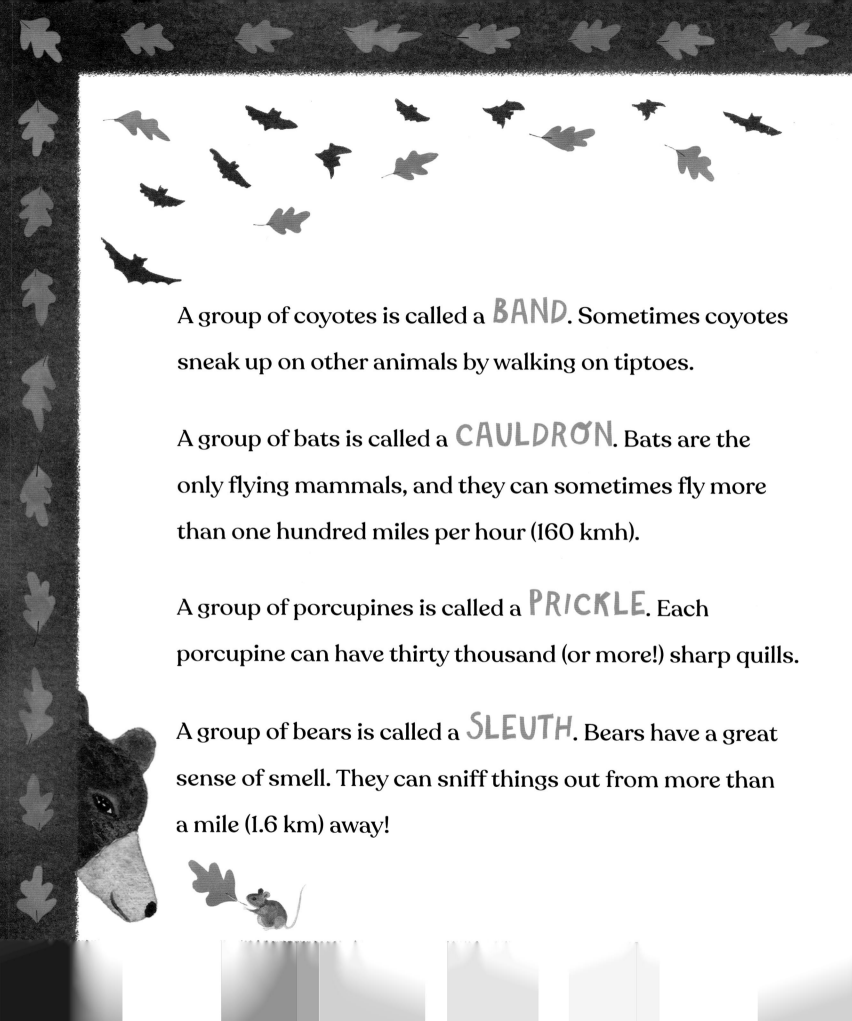

A group of coyotes is called a BAND. Sometimes coyotes sneak up on other animals by walking on tiptoes.

A group of bats is called a CAULDRON. Bats are the only flying mammals, and they can sometimes fly more than one hundred miles per hour (160 kmh).

A group of porcupines is called a PRICKLE. Each porcupine can have thirty thousand (or more!) sharp quills.

A group of bears is called a SLEUTH. Bears have a great sense of smell. They can sniff things out from more than a mile (1.6 km) away!